Hey Jack! Books

The Crazy Cousins
The Scary Solo
The Winning Goal
The Robot Blues
The Worry Monsters
The New Friend
The Worst Sleepover
The Circus Lesson
The Bumpy Ride
The Top Team
The Playground Problem
The Best Party Ever
The Bravest Kid
The Big Adventure
The Toy Sale
The Extra-special Group
The Star of the Week
The Book Buddies

First American Edition 2013
Kane Miller, A Division of EDC Publishing

Text copyright © 2012 Sally Rippin
Illustration copyright © 2012 Stephanie Spartels
Logo and design copyright © 2012 Hardie Grant Egmont
Design by Stephanie Spartels
Typesetting by Michaela Stone

First published in Australia in 2012 by Hardie Grant Egmont

For information contact:
Kane Miller, A Division of EDC Publishing
P.O. Box 470663
Tulsa, OK 74147-0663
www.kanemiller.com
www.edcpub.com
www.usbornebooksandmore.com

Library of Congress Control Number: 2012931655

Printed and bound in the United States of America
12 13 14 15 16 17 18 19 20
ISBN: 978-1-61067-124-8

Hey Jack!

The Robot Blues

By Sally Rippin

Illustrated by Stephanie Spartels

Kane Miller

A DIVISION OF EDC PUBLISHING

Chapter One

This is Jack.

Today Jack is in a
wobbly mood. He feels
funny in his tummy
and wobbly in his legs.

Jack has been invited
to a party. It is a
dress-up party for a
boy on Jack's soccer team.
The boy's name is Jem.
He doesn't go to
Jack's school.

Jack won't know anyone
at the party except
for Jem. That's why
he's feeling wobbly.

Jack has dressed up as a
robot from outer space.
He made his costume
himself.

This morning Jack
thought his costume
was awesome.
But now he thinks it
might look silly.

Jack worries that
all the kids at Jem's
party will have cooler
costumes than his.
Probably costumes from
a shop, not just ones
they made themselves.

4

"Hey, Jack!"

Jack hears his mom

call from downstairs.

"Time to go!"

Jack shuffles downstairs.

His costume is very

difficult

to walk in.

Jack can't bend

his legs all the way.

6

"Hell-o-Mom,"
Jack says in his best
robot voice.

Jack's mom laughs.
"Wow, that's some
costume!" she says.

Jack feels his face get
hot. He frowns.
"I don't want to
go to Jem's party
anymore," he says.

"Why not?" says

Jack's mom.

"Because my costume

is dumb," says Jack.

"I bet everyone else

will have cool

costumes, and they

will all laugh at me.

Just like you did!"

Jack's mom smiles.
"I was only laughing
at your funny voice,
Jack. Your costume
is great."

"Really?" asks Jack.

"Yep," Jack's mom says.
Then she puts on
a robot voice. "Ro-bot-
Jack-I-com-mand-you-
to-go-to-the-par-ty."

Jack feels his mouth **twitch** into a smile.

"All right, then," he says.

"Come on, let's go,"
says Jack's mom.

They drive to Jem's
house. Jack's mom stops
the car out in front.
Then she turns to
open the door.

"Wait!" says Jack. "I just
want to see what
the other kids are
wearing first."

So they sit outside Jem's
house in the car
and watch the other
kids arrive.

"Oh no!" says Jack.

"What's wrong?"
says his mom.

"Look," says Jack.
"That boy's got
a real Superman
costume. And look at
that boy. He's got a
Harry Potter costume.
A real one. Not a
homemade one.

My costume looks **stupid**. I knew I shouldn't have come!"

Chapter Two

Jack puts his seat belt
back on. He wants
to go home.

"I love your costume,"
says Jack's mom.

"And I'm sure there
will be lots of
superheroes and
lots of Harry Potters.
But no other robots
from outer space!"

Jack's mom is right.
Two more superheroes
and one more
Harry Potter walk
up to the front door.

Jack sighs.

Part of him wants

to believe his mom.

The other part
wishes she had just
bought him a
superhero costume.
They walk to the
front door. Jack hears
music playing and kids
laughing.
He feels his tummy
jump around
like a jumping bean.

Jem opens the door.

He is dressed

as Spiderman.

"Hey, Jack!" he yells.

"Cool costume!
Are you a robot?"

"Yeah... from outer
space," Jack mumbles
nervously.

"Awesome!" says Jem.
"Did you know there's a
prize for best costume?"

"Hey, that's great!"
says Jack's mom.

She tries to kiss Jack

goodbye, but he slips

away just in time.

"Have fun, honey!"

Jack follows Jem

down the hall to

the family room.

It's **full** of kids.

Jack takes a deep breath.

"Hey, everyone!"
Jem calls. "This is Jack,
my friend from soccer."

The room goes quiet.
All the kids stare at Jack.
Jack shrinks into
his costume.

Jem's friends come over.
Jack feels his heart
beating.

He is worried that

the kids are going

to laugh at him.

"Cool costume,"

says one boy.

Jack is surprised.

"Thanks," he says shyly.

"He made it

himself!" adds Jem.

"Wow!" says another boy.
"How did you make it?"

"Um, just boxes and paint
and stuff," shrugs Jack.

"I wish my mom let me make my costume," says another kid.

Jack grins **proudly**. He is beginning to feel very happy.

Chapter Three

"Hey, kids!" Jem's mom calls. "Time to vote for best costume! Everyone write down your vote, and put it in this box."

"I'll give out the prize after we have the cake," Jem's mom adds.

Jack votes for Jem's Spiderman costume.

"All right," says Jem's mom.
"Everyone has voted.
Who's ready for games?"

Everyone jumps
up and down in
excitement.
Everyone except Jack.
He can hardly walk
in his costume, let alone
jump! How is he going
to join in the games?

Maybe I should take it off,
Jack thinks. But he
needs help to take
off the boxes, and
he feels too shy
to ask Jem's mom.

First they play tag.
Jack is normally good
at party games, but today
he gets caught first
and has to sit out.

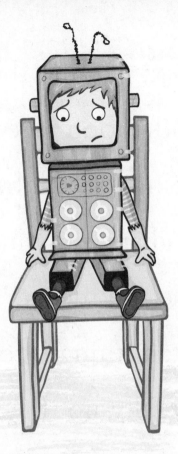

He will never win
a prize in his bulky
robot suit!

The next game is the egg-and-spoon race. Jack thinks he might have a chance at winning because the most important thing is to go carefully, not fast.

Jack puts his egg on a spoon. He lines up next to all the other kids.

Jem's mom calls,
"Ready, set, go!"

Everyone takes off.
Some kids go too fast
and **drop** their eggs
right away. But Jack
moves carefully,
concentrating on
his egg. Soon there
are only three kids
left in the race.

And Jack is in the lead!

The finish line is near.

Jack looks around.

He sees a boy coming
up behind him. The boy
is nearly beside Jack.

Jack walks faster.
He takes bigger and
bigger steps, until…
Rrrrriiiiiippp!
A piece of his costume
comes unstuck and
falls off.

Rrrrriiiippp!

Another piece falls off.
Jack trips over it and
tumbles down. His egg
smashes onto the grass.

Jack curls into a ball
on the grass and tries
to wipe away the tears
in his eyes.

Jem runs over. "Oh no!"
he says. "Your costume
is all broken!" He puts
his arm around Jack's
shoulders.

Jack takes a deep breath.

He doesn't want to cry in front of everyone.

"It doesn't matter about the costume," Jack says. "I can make another one easily."

"Why are you upset, then?" Jem asks.

"I wanted to win," Jack says in a little voice.

40

Jem laughs.

"That's OK!" he says.

"There will be plenty

more games after cake."

Jack starts to feel better. Now that his costume is broken, he will be able to run!

Jack and Jem go inside. Jem's mom brings his birthday cake to the party table. Everyone sings *Happy Birthday*. Jem's mom whispers something in Jem's ear.

Jem smiles. "Hey, everyone!" he says. "Mom counted the votes for the best costume. The winner is Jack!"

He hands Jack a prize wrapped up in paper. Jack **rips** open the paper. Something falls out. Jack bursts out laughing.

"Best prize ever!" he says
to Jem. He puts it on
right away.